I'M A
UNICORN

ISBN 978-1-339-03448-5

12 11 10 9 8 7 6 5 4 3 2 1   23 24 25 26 27 28

Printed in the U.S.A.   40

First Scholastic printing, September 2023

This book was typeset in Montserrat.
The illustrations were done in mixed media.

I'M A UNICORN

HELEN YOON

SCHOLASTIC INC.

I'm a unicorn.

See? This says:
uni means one
and *corn* means horn!

UNICORNS: FACTS

UNICORNS: FACTS & MYT

u•ni•corn
(yoo'-nĭ-korn')
From Latin: uni- (one),
cornu (horn)

And look:
I was born with just one horn!

I'm magical.

It says here, *Unicorns have hooves—check!—
are very beautiful—why, thank you!—
and poop rainbows.*

Rainbow poop, coming right up!

Hmm . . .

maybe unicorns are color-blind?

*Unicorns sparkle
in the sunshine
and twinkle
in the moonlight.*

*Unicorn manes flow like silk
and smell like peach candy.*

Unicorn footsteps sprout butterflies,
and their tears turn into lollipops. . . .

Am I . . .

not a unicorn?

I have no butterflies!

My tears aren't lollipops!

I'm not a unicorn!

Oh, no. REAL unicorns!
What are they going to think?

sniff
sniff

Excuse me.
Um, I think I owe you
an apology. You see,
all this time I thought
I was a unicorn. I've
been telling everyone
I was a unicorn.
But I don't think I'm
a unicorn.

sniff
sniff

Well, how many
horns do you have?

One.

Sounds like a unicorn to me.

Here. Eat this.
It always works for us.

I'm a unicorn!
I'm a unicorn!